Za-Za's
Baby Brother

Lucy Cousins

CANDLEWICK PRESS
CAMBRIDGE, MASSACHUSETTS

My mom is going to have a baby.

She has a big fat tummy. There's not much room for a hug.

Granny came to take care of me.

Dad took Mom to the hospital.

When the baby was born
we went to see Mom.

When Mom came home
she was very tired.
I had to be very quiet
and help Dad
take care
of her.

What a good boy.

Ooh, he's gorgeous.

I played by myself.

Dad was always busy.

Mom was always busy.

"Dad, Will you read me a story?"
"Not now, Za-Za. We're going shopping soon."

"Sorry, Za-Za, the baby's hungry and we have to go home."

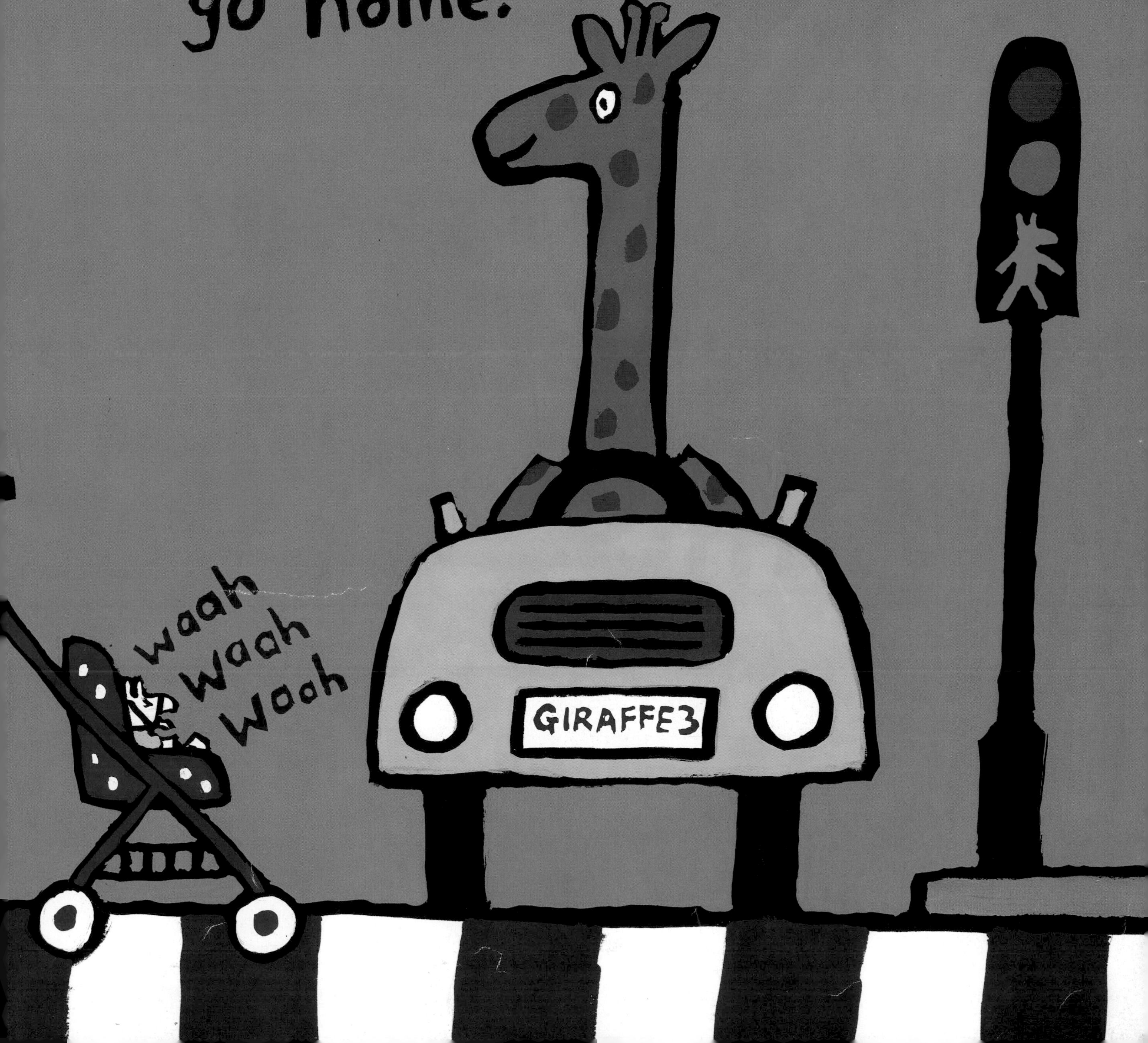

"Can I have my snack soon?"

"Yes, Za-Za."

So I hugged the baby...

and I pushed him...

and I
built him
a tower.

He was nice.
It was fun.

When the baby got
tired Mom put
him to bed.

Then I got my
hug...

and a bedtime story.